Let's wash up

Ira Wood

Rosen
REAL
READERS

Rosen Classroom Books and Materials
New York

Wash your hands often to stay healthy.

Wet your hands with warm water.

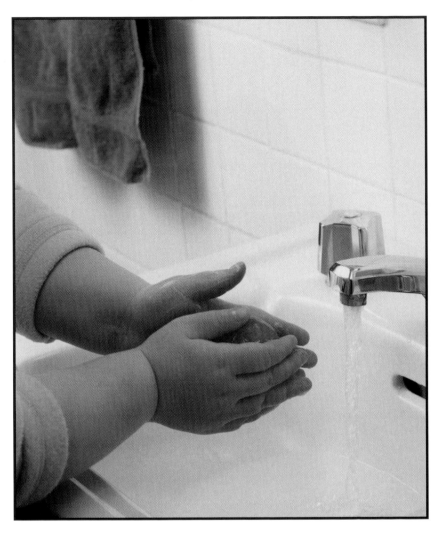

Put some soap on your hands.

4

Rub the soap all over your hands, even between your fingers.

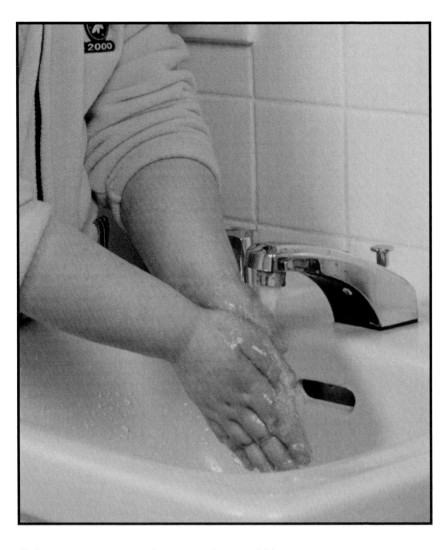

Rinse your hands with warm water.

Dry your hands with a towel.

Wash your hands before you eat.

Wash your hands after using the bathroom.

Wash your hands after playing outside.

Wash your hands after you
fingerpaint, too!

Words to Know

fingerpaint

soap

towel

wash